Fish for Supper

Fish for Supper

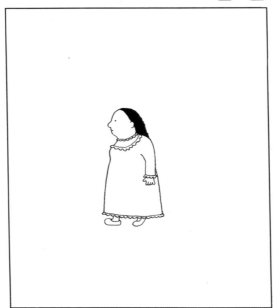

by M. B. GOFFSTEIN

Dial Books for Young Readers **New York**

Dial Books for Young Readers
A Division of E. P. Dutton
A Division of New American Library
2 Park Avenue, New York, New York 10016
Published simultaneously in Canada
by Fitzhenry & Whiteside Limited, Toronto

Library of Congress Catalog Card Number: 75-27598
Printed in Hong Kong by South China Printing Co. / First Pied Piper Printing 1986
COBE
10 9 8 7 6 5 4 3 2 1

A Pied Piper Book is a registered trademark of Dial Books for Young Readers,
a division of E. P. Dutton, a division of New American Library, ® TM 1,163,686 and ® TM 1,054,312

FISH FOR SUPPER
is published in a hardcover edition by Dial Books for Young Readers.
ISBN 0-8037-0284-1

To the Goffsteins

Fish for Supper

When my grandmother went fishing,

she would get up at five o'clock
in the morning

and make herself breakfast,

then clean up the dishes fast, fast,

and go down to the water
wearing her big sun hat.

With cans of worms and minnows,
some fruit for lunch,
bobbers, lines, hooks, and sinkers,

she rowed out in the rowboat

and stayed on the lake all day.

Over its sunlit waves and ripplets
she could see her yellow boathouse

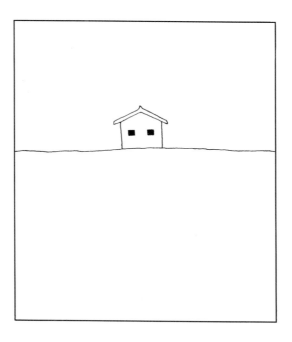

staring back at her with dark eyes
from the shore,

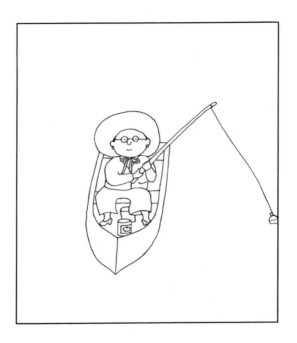

while she waited for the fish to bite.

She caught sunfish, crappies, perch,
and sometimes a big northern pike.

When she came home in the evening,

she cleaned the fish

and fried them in butter.

She took fresh rolls out of the oven,

put water for tea on the stove,

and sat down and ate very slowly,

taking care not to choke on a bone.

Then fast, fast, she cleaned up the dishes

and went to bed,

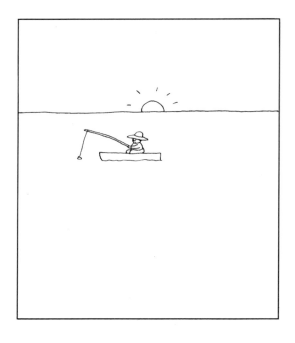

so she could get up at five o'clock
in the morning

to go fishing.